By Sophie Kinsella

What Does It Feel Like?

What Does It Feel Like?

A Novel

SOPHIE KINSELLA

The Dial Press
New York

Published in the United States by The Dial Press,
an imprint of Random House,
a division of Penguin Random House LLC, New York.

THE DIAL PRESS is a registered trademark and the colophon is
a trademark of Penguin Random House LLC.

Published in the United Kingdom by Bantam Press,
an imprint of Transworld, a division of
Penguin Random House UK, London.

LIBRARY OF CONGRESS CATALOGING-IN-PUBLICATION DATA

Names: Kinsella, Sophie, author.
Title: What does it feel like? : a novel / Sophie Kinsella.
Description: New York : The Dial Press, 2024.
Identifiers: LCCN 2024034027 (print) | LCCN 2024034028 (ebook) |
ISBN 9780593977569 (hardcover ; acid-free paper) |
ISBN 9780593977576 (ebook)
Subjects: LCGFT: Domestic fiction. | Novels.
Classification: LCC PR6073.I246 W47 2024 (print) |
LCC PR6073.I246 (ebook) | DDC 823/.914—dc23/eng/20240724
LC record available at https://lccn.loc.gov/2024034027
LC ebook record available at https://lccn.loc.gov/2024034028

Printed in the United States of America on acid-free paper

randomhousebooks.com

2 4 6 8 9 7 5 3 1

First U.S. Edition

Book design by Virginia Norey
Part title art: limousine by Oleg/stock.adobe.com,
Hospital room by aluna1/stock.adobe.com

To Henry

What Does It Feel Like?

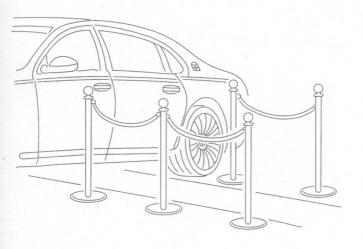

Before

How to Write a Book

"And now," says the nice interviewer from *Modern Woman* magazine, "how does it feel to be writing your seventh book?"

"It feels terrific," lies Eve. "I'm really thrilled to be working on it and I can't wait to share it with all my readers."

It's a nightmare. The words have jammed up for weeks and I don't know what I'm doing. Everything feels turgid; everything feels pointless. Why did I want to be an author again?

"Can you tell us anything about it?" probes the interviewer.

"Yes, it's a long family saga about a family called the Wilsons, set between the wars in a large country house."

"It sounds wonderful!"

"Well, thank you," says Eve, feeling unconvinced.

"We can't wait to read it! And now, I know our readers will want to ask: Do you have any advice for aspiring authors?"

"Yes," says Eve, who has answered this question about twenty-five thousand times and has therefore honed her thoughts. "I do, actually. My advice is to write the book you would like to read yourself. Visualize going into a bookshop and finding the perfect book. The book you would buy immediately. What does it look like? What's it about? What genre is it? Then write that book. And above all, write the truth. Write what you know and do it convincingly. I don't mean write nonfiction," she clarifies. "I mean write the truth about life, whatever genre you're in."

"Very wise advice. And now," says the interviewer, "moving on to your personal life, you have five children! How on earth do you manage to write?"

"Well, my husband is brilliant," says Eve honestly. "I couldn't do it without him. For example, today he's taken all the children off for a picnic so I can write."

"What a star!"

"He is. And we work as a team. I mean, it's always busy. We're always frantic. But it was our decision to have a large family and we love it."

"Well, thank you," says the interviewer. "That wraps it up. Thank you very much, and best of luck with the new book."

"Thank *you* very much," replies Eve. "Have a good day!"

She puts down the phone, deflates with a sigh, and looks unenthusiastically at her computer screen.

Back to the writing. She has an empty house; there's no excuse. The trouble is, she's lost any enthusiasm she once had for her plot, and there are still eighty thousand words to go.

The trouble is, I don't care about these stupid Wilsons anymore, muses Eve gloomily. *I don't care if Mr. Wilson loses his job, and I don't care if Harriet Wilson gets it together with the stable boy, and I don't even care if Britain goes to war.*

She contemplates making a cup of coffee—then reconsiders. Maybe she'll go and sit in a coffee shop and search for inspiration there.

✳

As she slams the front door behind her, she immediately feels lighter. *There* we are. She just needed a bit of fresh air. She saunters down the street, enjoying the sunshine and the alluring shop fronts coming into view. She's nearly into Wimbledon Village, the chi-chi high street with expensive shops and cafes on both sides of the road, and—

Oh my God.

She stops dead outside a boutique she's visited often before. The window is empty apart from one mannequin, wearing a dress, and as she looks at it, Eve's heart flips over.

It's not just any dress; it's a magical, silvery goddess of a dress, made of taupe silk and silver scalloped sequins. From the beaded shoestring straps to the tiny little train, it's perfect. It's an Oscar-winning dress. It would suit her perfectly. She just *has* to try it on.

The Wilsons and their crumbling country house have vanished from her mind as she ventures inside the shop and asks to try on the silver sequined dress.

"Of course," says the shop assistant, taking it off the mannequin. "It's by Jenny Packham. It's the only one left. Gorgeous, isn't it? What's the occasion?"

Oh God, thinks Eve. *What am I doing?* She doesn't have

any glitzy parties to go to. When would she ever wear anything like this?

She doesn't have an answer. She simply knows she has to try it on.

"No occasion," Eve says. "It's just a fabulous dress."

An occasion will present itself, she's sure.

As she slithers into the dress, she already knows it's a winner, and she's about to ask for help with the zip when her phone rings. Oh God, it's Nick. She's supposed to be writing and instead she's halfway into a dress she doesn't need.

"Hello?" she answers, aware that she already sounds guilty.

"Darling, so sorry to bother you when you're writing," comes his familiar resonant voice. "I just wondered how it was going and whether you wanted me to keep the children out for a bit longer?"

"No, don't worry," she says, her voice a bit shrill. "I'm . . . Actually, I've popped out to get some inspo."

"Great!" says her unsuspecting husband, and Eve blushes. Now she feels bad. But it's *such* a great dress. "Well, I won't distract you," he continues. "Good luck! See you later."

Eve heads out to the main shop floor and the shop assistant gasps. "You look amazing! You'll *have* to find an occasion to wear it."

"If you buy the dress, the occasion will come," says Eve mystically. "That's what I believe, anyway."

"So, are you going to buy it?"

"I think so. Can you do the zip up for me, please?"

As the assistant is doing up the zip, Eve knows she's going to buy it. At the same time, she's racked with guilt, because "buy dress" was definitely not on her to-do list today. Her to-do list consisted of one entry only: "write book." She has a deadline and a publisher waiting, not to mention her loyal readers.

After she's clambered out of the dress and the assistant is folding it up in sheets of tissue, Eve summons up her work-in-progress on her phone and runs her eyes over it. She hates every word. Then she summons up her latest Visa bill. She's not wild about that either. How can she have spent so much? She hasn't even been shopping recently. She scrolls down and up, then down again, trying to work out why she spent £39 in Fortnum and Mason. She never goes to Fortnum and Mason.

And then something weird happens. Her own words come back to her, loud and strong inside her brain.

Write the book you would like to read yourself. Write the truth about life, whatever genre you're in. Write what you know and do it convincingly.

What would she be interested in reading about? What does she know about? What are the truths she has learned about life?

A brand-new idea for a book has come to her, and it's so fresh and thrilling that she opens a document on her phone and starts typing rapidly, trying to get the idea down before she forgets it. She's going to take her own advice. She's going to write the truth. She's going to write the book she would love to read herself. She is going to write about what she knows.

Hey Big Spender by Eve Monroe
Chapter One

OK. Don't panic. As Dora Delaney stared at her Visa bill, she felt herself going through the stages of grief. Shock, anger, denial, bargaining, and eventually—very reluctantly—acceptance.

It could be worse, she thought, as she dismally surveyed her phone screen. Debt was just part of the circle of life, like art or tai chi, and must be accepted as such. Although had she really spent £99.50 at Sephora? What had she been thinking? And what was that £45 at North Face? She never went to North Face. Did she have amnesia?

Wait, had someone stolen her credit card?

Eve exhales, presses Save, then rereads her words with growing glee. This is more like it. *Write about what you know.* A book about shopping in London, not some tedious country-house saga. She's already thinking ahead: mapping out the chapters, imagining the dialogue, laughing at the jokes. This book will be fun to write. *Fun.* And she can't wait to get going. Scrap those stupid Wilsons and their tea dresses and their repressed upper-class manners. She wants to write something *real* and *now.*

"Did you want a copy of our catalog?" asks the assistant, who has been waiting patiently for Eve to finish.

"Yes, please, why not?" says Eve, and she feels a wave of conviction inside. Her new book will work. An occasion for a glittery dress will present itself. And this will always be her lucky dress, the dress she was wearing when she had her brand-new idea.

"And is there anything else you need?" asks the assistant. "Shoes? A wrap?"

"No, thank you," Eve says, beaming beatifically and reaching for her credit card. "I have everything I need."

Sophie Kinsella

Dear Eve:

Thank you so much for your manuscript of Hey Big
Spender. *And let me say first of all: wow! What a change
of direction for you! I love the comedy, Dora is hilarious,
and it all feels very fresh and of the moment.*

*I have shared the manuscript with a few members of
the team, and everybody else is just as excited as I am.
Well done! I look forward to talking more about how we
will publish this wonderful book. Meanwhile, congratulations again!*

Camilla Gray
Editor

Dear Eve:

*I just want to reiterate what Camilla said—I loved the
book and can't wait to get going on publicity ideas. This
one is going to be fun! And I just heard from Camilla that
Disney have optioned the book—congratulations!*

*We're already looking at some fun partnerships with
fashion shops and maybe an event or two. Would you be
up for that? Meanwhile,* Country Woman *have asked if
you would take part in their regular slot, "Me and My
Marriage." This is a lighthearted piece, and would be an
interview about your marriage, done by email or phone,*

whichever is convenient for you. Let me know if this is OK.

    Again, congratulations on Hey Big Spender *and here's to a publishing triumph—and the movie!*

Chloe Jarrett

Publicity Director

Country Woman
Me and My Marriage

Eve Monroe is the author of the novels *Just in Time, Paired Up,* and her upcoming book, *Hey Big Spender.* She is married to Nick and they have five children: John, Leo, Arthur, Reggie, and Isobel.

Where and when did you meet your husband?
We met on my first night at Oxford, at a party. We didn't get together straightaway, but within a few months we started dating.

When did you fall in love?
I heard Nick sing at a concert and that was it, done deal. His amazing voice blew me away and I just had to have him. So I pursued him blatantly and managed to get him interested in me. We've been together ever since.

Did you have a big wedding?
I was only twenty-one years old and super-romantic, so we had a big wedding with lots of music and I wore a massive meringue of a dress.

What is his best quality?
He has a very loud, generous laugh. He is my first reader and whenever he's reading my latest book I pace around downstairs, hoping I will hear him laugh.

What do you row about?
Clutter. I accumulate far too much stuff and Nick would be quite happy if the house were an empty box.

Would he be there for you if the going got tough?
Definitely. I can't imagine anyone I'd rather have at my side than Nick.

What do you hope for in the future?
A long and happy life together!

Eve presses Send and the interview disappears into the ether, but her thoughts and reminiscences remain. She was only eighteen years old when she met Nick, freshly up to Oxford. On her first night of term, she went to a party and there he was: a tall, interesting, fanciable kind of guy. She duly noted him, but the excitement of being at university distracted her, and that was that for the moment.

Until the Easter concert. His speaking voice as he introduced his number was charming enough—but then he began to sing, and his voice was solid gold. Full of sunlight, uplands, and strength. That was it. She was hooked.

Can you read character in a voice? Eve believes you can. She believes she heard the whole of Nick distilled into that melody. His goodness, his honesty, his sense of fun, his sense of humor. Everything.

So she began a campaign to win him. She got herself invited to drinks, she bumped into him strategically in the quad, she asked friends for help. She ended up on a sofa with him one night, edging closer and closer until he really had no choice but to kiss her. And so she got him.

Now she wants that to be the voice she hears when she dies.

On Top of the World

"OK, so this is your red-carpet pose," says Eve's film publicist, Brenda. "Legs crossed, hand on hip, elbow out, chin up."

"Right," says Eve, looking at herself in the mirror. She's in her glittery Jenny Packham dress—she *knew* she would need it one day—and there are diamonds winking at her ears, courtesy of earrings loaned to her by Boodles. On her wrist is a bracelet worth £80,000. She's not sure she's going to be able to think anything tonight except *Don't lose the £80,000 bracelet.*

As she's practicing different poses, her family piles into the room, all scrubbed up and in their best.

"Arthur's eaten all the chocolate from the minibar," reports Leo.

"So have you!" retorts Arthur.

"I had the freebies on the pillows," contradicts Leo. "You didn't want those."

"Yes, I did!"

"OK, leave it!" says Eve quickly. "No arguing today. You all look very smart, by the way."

"So do you, Mum," says John. "Super-glamorous."

"Thank you, darling." She laughs. "I do my best."

"OK," says Brenda. "The car's waiting downstairs. Everybody ready? Let's go!"

Their car is a sleek black SUV limo and as the family gets in, they all exclaim at the opulence of their surroundings.

"Free Coke!" says Reggie in delight, reaching for a can, and Eve, who would normally veto fizzy drinks, just laughs.

As they edge their way into Leicester Square, already there's excitement in the air. Searchlights are shooting up into the dark night, crowds are gathered, camera crews are lined up along metal railings, and beyond them is a glimpse of red carpet. It's like seeing the Yellow Brick Road. As Eve peers out of the window she spots Carrie Sanderson, the star of the film, looking petite and perfect in green sequins, and she feels a fresh flicker of excitement. This is really happening.

"Well, here we are!" she says, looking at her wide-eyed children. "Let's do this!"

And with that, they are out of the limo and being expertly led to the red carpet by Brenda.

"Eve!" calls Carrie Sanderson, spotting her and hurrying over. They embrace, cameras clicking all around, and Eve feels a wave of surrealism—she knows a movie star! Eve has always felt tall next to the petite Carrie, and now she's wearing such high heels she feels like a giant.

"We made it!" Carrie holds up a hand, and as they high-five, Eve remembers the endless days on set, the late nights, the takes after takes after takes, the hasty rewriting of lines.

We earned this party, she thinks. Although even now the work isn't done. She isn't here to relax, she's here to promote.

As though reading her thoughts, Brenda appears by her side.

"We're ready for your photo calls," she says. "First you on your own, Eve, then you with the family. Then you and Carrie, then both of you with the producer and director, OK?"

Eve walks awkwardly into place and begins the rigmarole of trying to look svelte for the cameras while another wave of disbelief washes over her. Is she, Eve Monroe, really posing for cameras on the red carpet? Her gaze travels beyond the lenses to the crowds packed behind the metal railings, some holding out books for her to sign—and she hears her own name being called, among all the others. It's all just bizarre.

Now the cameramen are shouting for her.

"Eve, over here!"

"Eve, love, this way!"

The flashes nearly blind her, and she clings desperately to her rigid pose, trying to make flattering angles with her hips and arms, wishing she'd practiced more in the mirror.

"Now," says Brenda, at her side once more. "One with all your family. People want to see your husband and the five kids."

Eve knows there is interest in her brood of children. Five kids. It's a lot, these days. It's a talking point. "What does it feel like to have five children?" people ask, and all she can say is, "The same as having one child, times five." The work is multiplied, the worry is multiplied, the joy is multiplied, the love is multiplied.

As her children assemble around her, Eve gives encouraging smiles all round.

"Now, everyone pretend we're a nice normal family," she says, quoting a comic sign that hangs in their kitchen, then turns her laser gaze on Reggie, aged nine. "And Reggie, *no* silly faces or rabbit ears. Stand up straight! Smile!"

"Over here!" photographers start shouting. "Kids! Look this way. Eve, to your right, please! Eve! Eve!"

Her family have done her proud, she thinks fondly, the boys in suits and Isobel in a pretty dress with silver Mary Janes. This will be something for her Show and Tell at school, anyway.

"Now ITN would like a word," says Brenda in her ear when the photos are finished. "Come this way."

She leads Eve to a camera crew and Eve follows, trying to stay in her red-carpet pose, just in case she gets snapped. She clamps her hand on her hip, keeps her legs crossed, and shuffles awkwardly along like a crab, wondering how on earth the movie stars manage to walk naturally.

"Eve!" A blond TV presenter greets her, holding a microphone and beckoning to a camera crew. "Antonia Horton from ITN. What does it feel like to have your book turned into a major Hollywood movie?"

"It feels surreal," says Eve. "The whole thing is just amazing and surreal."

"And are you happy with the movie?"

"Very happy. I think Carrie is hilarious."

"You were on set too, I believe?"

"Yes, for a few months. It was intense!"

"What an experience! And I see all your children are here with you too—so, can I ask you, Eve Monroe, best-selling author, how does it feel to have it all? The starry career, the five children, and now a movie!"

It feels lucky, thinks Eve at once. *I just feel super-uber-lucky, all the time.*

Of course she works hard—but she's also constantly aware of the good fortune she's had. She's lucky to have met Nick. She's lucky to have been fertile and had children. She's lucky that she's able to write. She's lucky her brain came up with the right idea at the right time and she was able to write *Hey Big Spender.*

Well done, you brilliant brain, she thinks—then draws breath to reply.

"I've been so incredibly fortunate, it almost seems like too much luck for one person," she says truthfully to Antonia Horton. "Now I'm just waiting for my luck to run out!"

After

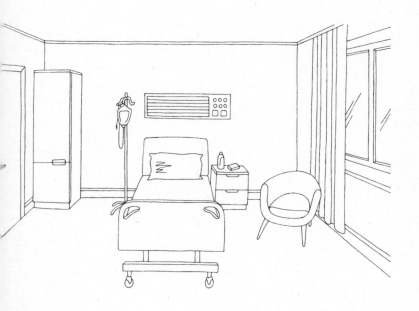

Can You Feel This?

Hands are coming toward her body, hands in tight blue plastic gloves, running gently up and down her arms.

"Can you feel this?" says a disembodied voice.

She's lying in bed, she realizes. *What's going on?*

"Do you remember your name?"

She tries to focus and eventually finds herself looking at the face of a nurse in green scrubs.

"My name is Eve Monroe," she says, slowly and cautiously. Her voice sounds blurry and indistinct to her own ears and her head aches. She reaches up to scratch her forehead and encounters a soft bandage, which seems to encase her whole head. Again: *What's going on?*

"Do you remember what day it is?" the nurse questions her again.

"Monday?" she hazards, having no idea.

"Wednesday. Do you remember what year it is? Do you remember the name of the prime minister?"

"It's 2022," she says, "and the prime minister is . . ." She digs around her mind fruitlessly. The prime minister. The prime minister. "Hugh Grant," she says triumphantly at last, then corrects herself. "No, he was ages ago, wasn't he? It's a woman now. But I can't quite remember her name."

"It's Rishi Sunak," says the nurse, kindly.

Right. Of course. Rishi Sunak.

"Now, tell me. Can you feel my hands rub up and down your legs?"

"Yes," she says.

"On both sides or just one?"

"Both," she says.

"Good. Can you squeeze my hand?"

"Yes."

"And with the other hand?"

Dutifully Eve squeezes.

"Can you lift your leg up and press against my hand?"

"I think so," says Eve, lifting her leg up, wondering why it feels so heavy.

"And the other one . . . Oh good, you're strong. You'll be up before you know it. But not quite yet. You still have a catheter in, so don't worry about that."

"OK," she says, not knowing what any of this means. There's a massive gap in her memory. Why is she here? What's happened? Was she in a car accident?

"OK, I'll see you in a while," says the nurse. "Are you eating OK?"

"She's eating fine," comes a masculine voice from above her head. Her husband, Nick, she realizes. "But she seems quite confused. It's like she has amnesia."

"Don't worry," replies the nurse. "That might be a short-term side effect. Tell your consultant if it carries on. But she should start remembering things naturally before too long."

"Nick, I can't move my head," says Eve in a voice that sounds cracked and scorched. "Can you sit where I can see you?"

"Of course." He appears and sits down on the hospital bed and she feels herself relax a smidge.

"Have I been unwell?"

"Yes," he says. "You had surgery. But now you're healing. You're doing brilliantly."

"I thought Hugh Grant was the prime minister," she says ruefully. "How could I be so dumb? I know he's the foreign secretary. . . . That's a joke," she adds, and Nick laughs.

"You've had a lot on your plate," he says. "Don't worry about it."

"What kind of surgery did I have?"

"You had a growth removed from your brain."

"A growth?"

"Yes, a growth, quite a big one. You saw it on a scan, do you remember? We all saw it together in the surgeon's office."

"No," she says, searching her brain. "No, I don't remember. When you say growth, do you mean . . ." She stops as her thoughts catch up with her. "Do you mean a tumor?"

"Yes, a tumor," he says after a pause. "It took eight hours to remove. But they got it all out, so that's great news."

"What . . ." She swallows. "What kind of tumor?"

There's a weighted pause, then Nick says, "Nobody knows for certain yet. It's being analyzed."

"Right," she says. "To see if it's . . ." and then she stops speaking.

Words start floating around her brain as though on a screensaver: medical words that she shrinks from even thinking. *Benign. Malignant. Cancer.*

But she doesn't say any of them aloud. She is numb, she realizes. She can't wonder, she can't ask more questions, she can't worry, she can't contemplate, she can't process. She can't feel anything at all.

They removed a growth from her brain and it took eight hours. How could it take eight hours?

She prods her emotions again. Still nothing.

Shock, she thinks. *I'm in shock. That must be it.*

"Knock, knock!" comes a cheery voice and in walks another nurse, this time in blue scrubs. "Just a quick check-over," she says. "Can you feel this?" Her hands run up and down Eve's arms. "And this? And this? Well done, you're in good shape!"

"Am I?" says Eve, ridiculously grateful for this affirmation.

"Oh yes, you're doing very well!"

She can feel everything on the outside, thinks Eve. She can feel the nurses, tickling her arms and tapping her legs and stroking her hands. But on the inside, where it really counts, she can't feel anything: not fear, not worry, not anxiety. There's nothing there at all, except those impersonal medical words, still floating around, no matter how hard she tries to dodge them.

She lies back and stares up at the white hospital ceiling, while the words go round and round her head. *Benign. Malignant. Cancer.*

Maybe, if she thinks hard enough, she can make one of them come true. She can influence the outcome. Like a manifestation. Or a prayer.

Benign. Benign. Benign, she thinks, using every brain cell she has. *Please. Please. Please.*

How to Walk with a Zimmer Frame

Eve doesn't understand it at all. What's going on?

She's upright, clutching on to two metal bars, and her head is spinning as though she's drunk six margaritas. She lifts a hand to her head and encounters only the softness of a bandage. Why is her head bandaged all over?

"Frame, step step," says a female voice to her left. Eve tries to look round, but her head swirls, and she feels she might fall over. She grips more tightly to the metal bars, wondering what to do.

"I'm dizzy," she says at last, unsure who she's speaking to. "Sorry, who are you? I seem to be having some problems with my memory."

"I am Yuliya, your physiotherapist," says a young woman, coming into view. "We are having a physiotherapy session and you are doing very well. Now we're going to try to move forward with the Zimmer frame again. Move the frame first, then walk forward. Frame, step, step."

Summoning all her strength, Eve moves the frame forward and manages to step with legs that feel like lead.

"I walked the red carpet," she says, having a weird flash of memory. "Years ago. In really high heels. That was hard too."

Why was she on the red carpet? she wonders. She must have been going to see a film.

"Well, there you go," says Yuliya. "You'll walk the red carpet again one day. Can you turn your head and look over your shoulder?"

Eve tries to swivel her head, but the motion brings on a rush of dizziness and nausea.

"No," she says desperately. "I can't move my head at all. Look, sorry, but what's wrong with me? Why am I doing this? I have a very patchy memory."

"You recently had brain surgery," says Yuliya. "Do you remember that?"

"No," says Eve in panic. "Why did I have brain surgery?"

"You had a tumor removed. Very successful surgery, all good. And now we are making you strong again. Your walking will improve, your balance will improve, everything will improve. Think positive. OK?"

"OK," says Eve obediently. Think positive. She can do that.

"Now you hold my hands, yes? And we'll walk without the frame. Left foot, right foot. Step, step, step, very good. Step step step, keep going."

"I can't," says Eve through gritted teeth. "I feel so *dizzy*. I'm going to fall over."

"Don't worry, I have you. You won't fall. But OK, maybe that's going too fast. Now we'll use the Zimmer frame again. Are you tired? Just think about that red carpet! Frame, step step. Frame, step step."

Eve feels like she's dragging two sacks of coal along the floor. What's wrong with her legs?

"Now we'll stop. Can you lift your hands from the frame?"

"What, stand on my own?" The feat seems impossible. Unthinkable. She unpeels one hand from the metal bar but doesn't dare release the other in case she falls over.

She's suddenly reminded of her children as adorable toddlers, learning to walk with wooden trolleys filled with blocks—which brings her to a new thought. Where are the children?

"The children," she says in a kind of gasping panic, grabbing the frame again.

"Children?" Yuliya says.

"I have five children. Where are they?" She feels like she used to in supermarkets, looking around, realizing the toddler has run off somewhere, fearing kidnappers, imagining the worst-case scenario.

But they're not toddlers anymore, she remembers. They're . . . How old are they? Come on, she knows this.

John, the eldest, is . . . twenty-one. Yes. And Isobel, the youngest, is ten.

She remembers her children's ages, but she still doesn't quite understand why she's standing in a hospital corridor, learning to walk again. Her whole life seems fractured, like a kaleidoscope.

"They're all fine. They send their love." It's Nick's voice, but she can't turn her head to see him.

"Please will you move to where I can see you?" she asks, and in a moment he comes into view, his smiling face so familiar and lovely that her eyes smart with tears. Has he been there the whole time?

"I'm in hospital," she says, just to get things straight. "I had a brain tumor," she adds with a fresh rush of memory.

"Yes. You're in hospital and you had a brain tumor, but it was removed."

"Can't the children visit?"

"They did visit," he says carefully. "Don't you remember?"

Eve feels as though she's going mad.

"Yes," she lies. "Of course I remember. I wouldn't forget seeing the children." She meets eyes with her husband. He doesn't look fooled.

"I can't walk," she says. "It's crazy."

"Yes, you can! You're really improving."

"This is an improvement?" she says, trying to hide how aghast she feels. "Good God."

"You're doing brilliantly." He comes to hug her tight. "You're so much stronger than you were."

"This is a marathon, not a sprint," chimes in Yuliya, nodding. "You're making progress every day. Well done!"

"It's like when you write your books," says her husband, squeezing her hand. "You get there little by little. Chapter by chapter."

Her books. The thought floods Eve's mind like a tsunami. She writes books. All those words, those chapter headings, those edits, those bestsellers. Of course. She did all that. It seems like some sort of miracle.

"I write books," she says aloud, in slow, wondering tones, almost as though reminding herself. "I write books and I had a brain tumor and I walk with a Zimmer frame."

"That's about it," says Nick, laughing.

"OK." For a moment she lets her thoughts settle. Tears are rising again, hot at the back of her eyes, but she swallows hard again and again, determined not to let a single drop fall. She is where she is, bizarre as it may seem. And there's only one way out. There's only one option. With renewed vigor, she moves the frame forward a few inches on the vinyl floor, then drags her legs along in a semblance of walking.

"Frame," she says, her voice a little husky. "Frame, step step. Frame, step step. Frame, step step."

WhatsApp

Eve's Family Support Group

Hi Nick, I just wanted to let you know that the children had a lovely day today—we all did a jigsaw together and made scones. Sending all love to Eve and you of course. Marjorie xx

Hi Nick, how's Eve getting on? Just to let you know, that's fine about having Isobel, Reggie, and Arthur next weekend, we'll have a blast. The girls love having their cousins to stay!! Do they like lasagna?? Sending you both all our best love. Imogen xxx

Hi Nick, I've been doing some research on brain tumors and enclose a few articles that might be interesting. I am also very happy to come to any doctor's appointments if Eve is still too fragile. My three have been making get-well cards for Eve, so I will pop them in the post, meanwhile much love from us all. Ginnie xxx

The Walkers

Eve clings on to Nick's arm as they walk along the city street. She feels frail today, and her legs are somehow both heavy and wobbly. But that's because she's been in hospital, she reminds herself. Yes. For something to do with her head. She had an operation. That's right. It's all coming back to her. Her head was bandaged and for a while it felt heavy and alien, as though it had been replaced by a metal robot's head.

But apart from that, she's fine. Isn't she?

She can't really remember. At the back of her mind,

something is nagging at her, something that feels like it might be important . . . but she can't recall it now.

"Good for you, love!" calls a builder from a nearby building site. "You're getting stronger every day."

"How does he know?" she says, astonished. "Have we been out here before?"

"A few times," says Nick, squeezing her hand. "And he's right. You *are* getting stronger every day. So—you don't remember coming out for any other walks like this?"

"Not really." She pauses. "Maybe if I think hard."

They walk on a few more steps and a light flurry of snow hits them in the face.

"Snow!" exclaims Eve. "What date is it?"

She has no idea even what month it is, she realizes. But there again, she's never been good at dates. It doesn't mean anything.

"It's December the twentieth," says Nick.

"Christmas!" She stops dead. "Christmas! We need to get presents! The children! Have they done their lists? Where *are* the children?" she adds, in a flurry of panic.

"The children are having a lovely time with your mother and the presents are bought and wrapped," he says patiently. "The children did lists and we ordered them together. You sat up in bed and we did it on the iPad."

"Right." Eve roams around the recesses of her mind, but draws a blank. "I don't remember."

"It doesn't matter." He squeezes her hand. "Just don't worry about it. Christmas will be fine. You'll be home!"

"Home!"

Eve is about to ask how long it is since she's been at home when a sound distracts her. It's a sound deep inside her head and she doesn't like it.

"Are you OK?" asks Nick as she stops dead in the street.

"My head is ticking," she says. "It's the weirdest thing, Nick, it sounds like a fast electric alarm clock ticking away in my brain."

"That's just your brain knitting back together," he says reassuringly. "You've heard it before. It's common after the kind of surgery you had. We asked the doctor."

"It's freaky." She makes a face.

"I'm sure it is. But don't worry about it. Oh, I spoke to your mother," he adds. "She sends you her love and of course says she hopes you feel better." He pauses cautiously. "You know you've been unwell?"

"Of *course* I know I've been unwell," she says as robustly as she can, because this conversation is secretly unnerving her. She keeps searching her head for clues, but comes across great gaps instead. What's happened to her brain? It feels patchy and incompetent and not like herself at all.

"Do you remember the words to 'O Come All Ye Faithful'?" asks Nick. "Only we sang it yesterday, as we were walking along."

"Of course I remember 'O Come All Ye Faithful'!" she says with a laugh, and draws breath to sing. "*O come all ye faithful . . . Long live our noble king . . .* No, wait." She stops. "That's wrong. Stupid."

"Never mind," says Nick. "It's only a carol. I just wondered if it had stuck."

"I can remember a carol, for God's sake!" says Eve in frustration and, mustering all her mental energy, begins singing again. "*O come all ye faithful . . . Glory to the newborn king . . .*" She stops doubtfully. "Is that right?"

"Take a break," says Nick. "Don't push yourself. It's only a carol. It doesn't matter."

"But I want to *remember*," says Eve desperately. "What's

wrong? I never . . ." She trails off as memories suddenly crowd her brain.

"Hang on. Did I need a Zimmer frame?" she asks, appalled by the idea.

"Yes, you used a Zimmer frame for a while," says Nick matter-of-factly.

She is silent for a moment as it all slowly returns to her. The huge effort just to move an inch. The voice of the physiotherapist as she struggled forward. Her arms trembling with effort. Her head numb with disbelief that she—the sporty one, the lover of high heels—should need a *Zimmer frame* to walk.

"I remember that now," she says. "And I remember that time I fell over." More images are filling her brain. *CALL, DON'T FALL.* The phrase flashes into her head. She can see it written in Sharpie on pieces of paper, stuck up on the walls of her room. Her hospital room.

Now she's remembering the nurses. The meals; the wide shower with its red plastic call button; the meds cart. She's been in hospital for a while, she realizes.

"*Call, don't fall,*" she says out loud, and Nick gives a wry laugh. "Yes, indeed. You had to learn that one. You kept forgetting you couldn't walk."

"I pulled over that piece of hospital machinery," she says, recalling the entire incident in a fresh flood of memory. "I thought I could walk to the bathroom. I got that awful bruise on my arm."

"You did." Nick's mouth twitches. "You had lots of nurses very worried. In fact, I'm only allowed to take you out now because I've promised to hold on to you tightly. They don't trust you to behave."

She laughs, thankful to have something to smile at, even if it is her own pratfall.

"But I can walk now."

"Yes. You learned again. You did brilliantly."

"I had an operation, didn't I?" she says, trying to sound matter-of-fact, as though she remembers everything.

"Yes. And it went very well. So that's a positive."

Other things aren't so positive, he thinks. *But you haven't asked about those. Not yet.*

"Another carol?" he suggests. "'Silent Night'?"

As they walk to the corner, they sing an approximation of the carol together, arm in arm, laughing when they go wrong. But even though she's enjoying the little sing-along, Eve can't focus on it. She keeps losing her grip on the words, and besides, that nagging feeling is back. What *is* it? She feels like she needs to know something, like there's a missing piece to this jigsaw. . . .

"Nick?" she says at last, cutting into his rendition of "Silent Night."

"Yes?" He stops singing; looks down at her.

"What's wrong with me?"

For a full minute, Nick stares at his wife, unable to speak. It comes every time, this moment. This terrible, impossible moment. And each time, it seems to come sooner; her eyes seem wider; her incomprehension seems greater.

You have incurable cancer, my beautiful Eve. But you keep forgetting and I have to keep reminding you and these are the hardest moments of my life.

He will tell her the truth, as he has told her on every walk. And he will deal with her shock, as he has done on every walk. He will deal with her questions, her tears, her worries, her fears for the children. For all of them.

But not just yet. *Let me have just a few minutes,* he thinks. *Just a few more minutes of happy innocence.*

"Before we get to that," he says, "what about 'O Little Town of Bethlehem'? Do you remember that?"

"I must do!" She draws breath and sings. "*O little town*

of Bethlehem . . . the silent stars go by . . . No, that's wrong. . . . Wait, I've got an idea." Her face brightens. "You print me out the words of all the carols and I can relearn them by Christmas."

"Of course. Good idea. I'll give you a printout," says Nick.

He'll give her the printout he's already given her and that she's discarded in frustration three times now, sitting up in her hospital bed, wailing, "I can't learn these sodding carols!"

"Well, shall we just walk for a bit?"

"Yes. Let's just walk for a bit."

So they carry on, the pair of them, arm in arm, snowflakes flurrying around them. Occasionally he glances down at her and she smiles back. Her eyes are already vague again—he can tell her thoughts are scattering away—but her steps are firm and steady. And right at this moment, he thinks, right at this exact, magical moment, he could almost think that nothing was wrong at all.

Dear Daddy

Granny is letting me use her email. Can I buy a new pencil case? I miss Mummy, when is she coming home?

Izzy xxxxxxxxxxxxxxxxxxxxxxxxx

You Must Remember This

"Would you like some lunch?"

Eve opens her eyes from dozing to see her husband, sitting on the end of a hospital bed that she appears to be in.

"Are you awake now?" he says. "Are you hungry?"

Searching for clues, Eve looks around her surroundings. Her gaze falls on a white board, on which someone has helpfully written:

Today is Tuesday.
Nurse for the day: Suzi.

Aims for the day: Have a happy day:)
And remember: CALL, DON'T FALL.

Hospital. She's in hospital.

She had surgery. Yes. That's right.

Her eye falls on a collection of homemade Get Well cards on her tray table and she picks one up. It is from Izzy, her ten-year-old, her baby, and is painted with her unmistakable artistic flair. *Get well soon Mummy* is printed carefully inside, followed by, *I miss you, love from Izzy xxx*

Eve's heart contracts painfully. When did she last see her children? It feels like it was an age ago. Weeks. Years.

Where are they now, anyway?

Thoughts and questions are piling into her head, as if her head is a computer and it's loading up again after a long sleep.

Call, don't fall. That's because she keeps falling over. That's how she got the bruise on her arm.

She looks at her hand. There is a cannula going into a vein, taped in place on her skin. *For the steroids,* she thinks automatically, then blinks. Steroids?

"Where are the children?" she asks aloud, her voice croaky.

"They're being looked after by your mother."

"How long have I been in hospital?"

"A good while now."

Her head feels heavy, she realizes. Heavy and kind of awkward. And her face feels tight, as though the skin has been stretched taut.

Her eyes stray to the single mattress squeezed into the room, the familiar blue T-shirt folded up on the pillow. "Have you been sleeping here?" she asks.

"I've been here the whole time," says Nick.

"The whole time?" she says in disbelief.

"I wasn't going to leave you, you silly girl." He reaches out and squeezes her hand. "And the children are fine. Having a whale of a time with your mother, by all accounts."

"Right."

She rubs her head and feels nothing but soft bandage. "What do I look like?"

"Have a look," says Nick, gesturing at the bathroom. "D'you want a hand?"

She leans gratefully on his arm as she toddles into the bathroom and faces the mirror.

Oh my God.

She has a turban of white bandage. Her face is sallow and puffy. She wouldn't recognize herself at all, if it weren't for the familiar eyes peering doubtfully back at her.

Another flood of memory pours into her mind. "I had an operation on my brain," she says slowly, "and then we had a meeting with the doctor, and we looked at my scan on the computer together. It's coming back to me now."

"You remember all that?" Nick sounds pleased. "Maybe you're getting your memory back. Yes, we met with your surgeon and we talked about your operation. It was a great success. Remember that?"

"I was in a wheelchair," she says in sudden astonishment.

"Yes, you needed a wheelchair. Do you remember the children visiting?" he adds, as Eve turns and heads back to the bed.

"No," she says. "Wait, yes. Isobel gave me this, didn't she?" She reaches for the little furry rabbit on her tray table, which had been puzzling her.

"She bought it herself," says Nick. "She said, 'Mummy can't be in hospital without a teddy.' So we went teddy shopping."

Eve gives the little white rabbit a tender hug, then places it prominently on her duvet.

"Eve . . ." Nick pauses, his face serious. "What else do you remember of the meeting with the doctor?"

"I remember they took out a growth." A big hard lump of certain knowledge lands in her brain, like an iron bar falling to the floor. "And they said it might be cancer."

"Yes."

There is a long, long pause, then Nick says, "Eve, my darling, I have some news. They've analyzed the growth and it *is* cancer."

"Right," she says, and feels hot tears spring to her eyes before she can stop them. She takes a big breath and exhales sharply, gathering all her strength. Cancer. OK. That's a big piece of news. But she's not going to feel sorry for herself, she decides fiercely. She's just not.

"OK. I've got cancer. Well, it is what it is. Will I have chemotherapy? Or radiation therapy? Or anything like that?"

"You'll have both."

She feels flattened for a moment. As though a car has driven into her. Cancer. She's a cancer patient.

But then, within seconds, her natural optimism surfaces.

"Oh well," she says as firmly as she can. "Never mind.

People have cancer. It's not the end of the world. They have cures for cancer these days."

"Yes, for a lot of cancers they do have cures."

There's an odd expression on Nick's face, and she feels a fearful tremor rumble deep inside her. There's a big, crucial question she wants to ask—but at the same time, she doesn't want to ask. She wants to know, but she doesn't want to know.

She chooses a different question instead.

"What kind of cancer have I got? Does it have a name?"

"You had a grade four glioblastoma. They got it all out, so now we have to hope it doesn't come back. That's what the chemotherapy and radiotherapy will be for. You'll be having them as soon as we get to the other side of Christmas."

"Grade four glioblastoma," echoes Eve carefully. The words feel vaguely familiar. "Have you told me this before?"

"A few times," says Nick, "but you sound more alert now. Maybe you'll remember this conversation."

"Knock, knock! Occupational therapist here!"

A woman in a brown uniform comes bustling in and beams at Eve. "I'm Maureen. We've met before, but I know you have issues with your short-term memory."

"I'll leave you," says Nick. "We'll come back to this conversation. I'll go and get a coffee and make a few calls. Will you be OK?"

"We'll be fine," says Maureen. "You go and do your thing."

For the next half hour, Eve obeys the instructions of Maureen, which takes her full concentration. She walks, she turns, she attempts unsuccessfully to stand on one leg, she visits the bathroom, she walks down the corridor clutching Maureen's arm and makes herself a cup of tea.

"Very good!" exclaims Maureen at the end of the session. "You've improved massively. You'll be able to leave hospital soon."

She scribbles some notes on her clipboard, then leaves—and Eve is alone.

She has cancer. It's surreal.

"I have cancer," she says out loud to see how it sounds. It sounds unbelievable.

She opens her iPad and goes to the browser. Carefully she types into the search box —

Grade 4 glioblastoma.

Within seconds, the results have appeared. She clicks and reads, then clicks on another page and reads, then clicks, reads, reads, reads, trying and failing to find a different answer, not believing what she's reading.

> Rare, incurable cancer...
> ...most aggressive form of brain tumor...
> ...virulent and deadly...
> ...unfortunately no cure...
> ...very poor prognosis...
> ...terminal...
> ...despite initial treatment with surgery, radiotherapy, and chemotherapy, glioblastoma virtually always recurs...
> ...Only 25 percent of patients survive more than one year...
> ...Average survival time is 12–18 months...
> ...Median adult survival time after diagnosis: 14 months.

As she finally looks up, she feels weak. She feels like she is falling down a deep, bottomless well. She can't die after fourteen months. She has five children. Isobel's only ten; she needs looking after. They all need looking after.

Tears are running silently down her face as she stares

at the iPad screen. Did she know this information already? Did she forget? How could she forget this?

Fear is clenching her spine, but she has to be brave. She has to be optimistic.

But, *fourteen months*. And that's the average. Is she average? Is she above average? Is she below average?

Almost gibbering in panic, she grabs her phone and sends Nick a text.

I googled glioblastoma. Xx

And almost at once, as though he was waiting, his reply comes into her phone.

Oh, my beautiful Eve. I'm coming.
Xxxxxxx

Good Job!

The cognition therapist is called Connie, and today Eve has remembered that fact, which already feels like a major triumph.

"Hi, Connie," she says, eager to show off her excellent memory for names. "How are you?"

"I'm good, thanks," says Connie, who is a cheerful American with cropped red hair and an energetic demeanor. "How are you?"

This is a tricky question to answer, Eve thinks. Does she answer big picture or small picture? Big picture: "I have incurable cancer, thanks for asking." Small picture:

"I feel fine today, apart from the knowledge that I am so cognitively impaired I need special therapy."

In the end, she distills all the possible answers into a platitude.

"Fine, thanks!" she says, trying to match Connie's enthusiasm, and Connie beams.

"Great! Now, to begin today's session, I have a few pictures for you to look at. See if you can tell me what they are and what they're used for."

She opens one of her folders and shows the contents to Eve. It is a line drawing of an object and Eve is almost certain she knows what it is. But the word won't come to her.

"Just describe the item as best you can," prompts Connie gently.

Eve stares at the line drawing, feeling frustrated. "It's a . . . You wear it and it has sleeves and . . ." She's run out of impetus.

"And what's it called?"

"A bag," guesses Eve.

"A shirt," says Connie kindly.

"A shirt," says Eve quickly. "That's what I meant. A shirt. You use it for wearing."

"Yes, you do!" exclaims Connie brightly. "Good job! Now, what about this one?"

This picture is easy and Eve answers with alacrity, feeling pleased with herself.

"A chair. You use it for being on. Sitting on."

"Good job!" exclaims Connie as though Eve has cracked quantum theory. "And this?"

"A pen," says Eve promptly, feeling a surge of triumph. "You use it for drawing. And for writing."

"Good job! And this one?"

Eve stares at the picture, dumbfounded.

"It's a . . . a . . . a device." Eve feels as though she's dredged the word up from heavy mud in her brain. "A device for . . . temperature. No, I don't mean that. For . . . measure. Tell the measurement," she concludes hopelessly, aware that she can't even speak properly, let alone identify this mystery object.

"It's a sextant," says Connie kindly.

A sextant? Did she ever know what a sextant was?

"And this picture?" Connie flips the page and Eve stares at the drawing.

"There's a horse," she says slowly, again feeling as though she's hauling up the words from somewhere deep and murky. "And they have the things on their eyes. The cover things."

"Do you know the name?"

Eve is silent. She doesn't know the name. Did she ever know the name?

"You know I'm a writer?" she says at last, in despair. "I have to know what words mean, or I can't make a living."

"You've improved a lot," says Connie. "Don't beat yourself up. You've been through so much. So are we giving up on this one? Have another look."

"Horse things," says Eve hopelessly. "That's all I can give you."

"Blinkers," says Connie.

"*Blinkers,* that's right."

I am an Oxford graduate, thinks Eve. *I got a first in PPE. And now all my words have disintegrated in my brain. Or maybe the surgeon took them out by mistake.*

"Now let's move on to our drawing exercises." Connie produces a piece of paper and a pen and hands them to Eve. Then she opens another folder. This one is red. And Eve knows it is the one full of scary drawings that she has to copy. She was never any good at drawing and now she's beyond remedial.

"Can you draw this shape?"

That shape? That huge and intimidating shape with zigzags and bobbles and lines everywhere?

She picks up a pen with a hand that feels shaky. Can she even draw a straight line?

Eve has coached her children through nonverbal reasoning exercises to get into brainy schools. She should know how to do this, but the idea of drawing even one line feels daunting.

"Just do your best," says Connie encouragingly.

Eve begins to draw, but she can't control the pen at all. It staggers and lurches on the page, and the result looks clumsy and all over the shop.

"Good job!" exclaims Connie, as though Eve has just drawn the *Mona Lisa*. "Let's try something else. Can you write your name?"

Of course she can write her name, thinks Eve firmly. She has to use mind over matter here. Of *course* she can write her name.

But the letters are wobbly and uneven, like the printing of a toddler.

"I used to sign books," she says, her voice sounding slurred to her own ears. "Lots of books. Thousands of books, really fast. And now I can't even write my name."

"Be gentle with yourself. You're doing so well, I'm going to push you a little. Can you draw the shape you just drew from memory? Here's another piece of paper."

From memory?

Eve stares at the blank sheet in terror. There was a bobble and a zigzag, that's all she can remember.

Using all her effort, she draws a bobble, a zigzag, and a few random straight lines.

"Good job!" exclaims Connie.

"Was it right?" asks Eve in hope.

"Not exactly right," says Connie, showing Eve a drawing that is nothing like Eve's attempt. "But some of the elements were correct. And you're making so much progress. Let's move on to blocks."

Eve's heart sinks. Not the blocks again. She was never any good at spatial awareness, and these blocks have defeated her every time.

"Here you are." Connie produces a quantity of triangular plastic blocks. "Can you make me a big triangle with these blocks?"

"I can try," says Eve, knowing already she will fail. She has grown to hate plastic blocks and wishes they could be banned. But she is committed to this therapy, so she will try again and again, and Connie will exclaim "Good job!" whatever she produces.

And the blocks will taunt her with their shiny cheerfulness and refuse to fall into shape, and she will wonder what her children would say if they could see her now, sweating and breathing hard, struggling to make a triangle.

WhatsApp

Eve's Family Support Group

Welcome home Eve!! Have a lovely reunion, the children have been looking forward to it!
Mum xxx

Welcome home Eve!!!!! Sending you all our hugs and kisses and looking forward to visiting on Saturday
Ginnie xxxxxx

Welcome back home Eve!!! Can't wait to see you!! Meanwhile get lots of rest and take it easy
Imogen xxx

I Don't Really Need
a Carer

Hello, lovely to meet you, Helen, come on in. This is the kitchen and this is the sitting room and this is the bedroom. I don't really need a carer, but my husband is away on business and he worries about me.

Yes, I've had surgery and now I'm on chemo and radiation therapy. I have to remember to take the right pills at the right time, that's the main thing. But other than that, I'm fine. I don't really need a carer.

My husband is very protective and, to be honest, he's overreacted. I'll be an easy job for you, because I don't really need any help. But it'll be nice to have some company.

Yes, it all kicked off before Christmas. At first I was just really wobbly and then I kept falling over. So they scanned my brain and found this tumor. I had brain surgery and then loads of rehab. But I'm so much better than I was. I really don't need a carer.

Let me show you around the kitchen. Tea and coffee? Yes, of course, just here.

Oh.

Sorry, not there. Here.

I just sometimes get confused about the cupboards. It's no big deal. They took a big chunk of my brain out and sometimes I get memory lapses.

Cook me supper? Wow. Well, that would be very helpful, thank you! I feel very spoiled. But I don't need it, really.

Yes, sorry, that saucepan is bust. My fault, I put an egg on to boil and forgot about it and it boiled all the way through. Stupid of me, really.

I think that's when my husband first called the agency. He gets worried that I can't cope on my own. But as I say, it was an overreaction. I don't really need a carer. Yes, chicken would be lovely. There's some in the fridge, I think. Oh, you know that already. Oh, you discussed supper with my husband? He is brilliant. I don't know what I would do without him. But he's gone to Ireland on work. Yes, he didn't want to go, but life goes on, you know?

Yes, don't worry, I'm happy to talk about it. The diagnosis was glioblastoma grade four, so that wasn't great. But I had surgery and they got the whole tumor out, so fingers crossed.

Oh God. I'm so sorry, I've forgotten your name already.

Helen. Yes. Helen. I can remember that. Helen. Sorry. I think when they took the chunk of brain out, they took out my short-term memory with it. But I'm fine, really.

Yes, radiation and chemo. Temozolomide. You have to remember not to eat at certain times when you're on this chemo, but luckily my husband reminds me, otherwise I would just eat a biscuit by mistake. I know. Easy to do. Yes, I love sweetcorn. Thank you so much!

It's quite a full-time job, this being-ill business. Remembering to take the right drugs at the right time, and going to radiotherapy and having all these blood tests and MRI scans. I haven't written anything for ages. I'm a writer, in case you didn't know. Oh, you did. Oh, really? Thank you so much! I'm glad you enjoyed it.

How long are you staying tonight? What, you're staying over? Wow, well, that's very helpful. I hardly ever fall over anymore, but I suppose to be on the safe side . . . OK, I'll call. Yes, I promise.

Yes, I do have a drug regime before bed. Well, that would be helpful. Oh, you've got a list from the agency? Well, that's brilliant.

But don't worry, I turn in very early these days. I'm asleep by nine o'clock and I don't wake up till eight. Yes, my husband usually gets the children to school, but they're with my mother today, as he's gone away.

Broccoli? Yes, I'd love some. I'm trying to eat really healthily at the moment. Give myself every chance.

You had another patient with glioblastoma? Wow. What are the chances? Oh, really? Was he? Well, I'm glad I'm not the only one with memory loss.

He was also on temozolomide? Wow, snap. Yes, it does make me feel sick. But I have a drug to help with that. You take one drug and then you have to take another drug, that seems to be the rule. Anyway, I'm glad I'm not the only one to get side effects.

Yes, rice would be lovely, thank you so much!

So why aren't you with that patient now?

Oh right.

Right.

Right. I'm sorry. That's— Yes. It must be difficult for you.

When was that, then?

Do you know how many months after diagnosis before he . . . ?

A year.

Wow.

Not long.

No, don't worry, I'm fine. I sometimes get watery eyes. Well, I'm two months post diagnosis and I'm doing fine so far. Onwards and upwards, that's what I say. You have to keep cheerful. And I have the children, they distract me. Oh yes, yes, please do go ahead and serve up. This is a real treat, having my supper cooked for me, but really, it's quite unnecessary. Would you like some? Oh, you bring your own food. Sensible of you.

Oh, that bruise? Yes, I suppose it is quite big. If I went out, people would think my husband was beating me up! I got it when I tripped in the shower. Stupid of me. It was just a slippery floor. Oh, the other bruise? That was when I went to the loo one time. I just lost my footing and caught my face on the sink. Stupid of me.

Yes, OK, I promise, I'll ring the bell. No, really, I can shower on my own, but I don't mind being escorted there, if you really feel . . .

And if I trip up on my way to the bathroom in the night or anything, I'll call for you. Yes. I really promise.

But I'm sure everything will be fine.

No, I really am. Because, as I say, I don't really need a carer.

Scrabble

From the outside, they probably look like a normal family, thinks Eve. If you glanced in through the window, you'd see a normal, happy family, gathered around a Scrabble board on the kitchen table.

Only as you came closer might you notice the expressions on everyone's faces and suspect something was amiss. Because they look variously tense, grim, tearful, disbelieving, and shell-shocked. She feels a bit shell-shocked herself, to be truthful. It's out. Finally, after all the agonizing and debating and worrying, it's out. All the family knows.

"Right," says Nick, and it's only from the faintest tension in his voice that she would have known anything was wrong. "Everyone take seven tiles. OK, Izzy? Take seven tiles and pass the bag along."

"Can you still come and see my play?" asks Isobel in a wobbly voice.

"Of course I can come and see your play," says Eve. "You won't stop me! I'll be in the front row, waving and cheering!"

"Thanks, Izzy," says John, taking the bag.

He looks less shell-shocked than Izzy, but then the news was not news for him. They've kept the three older brothers in the loop all the way along, then worked toward telling the younger ones at a good time, with the whole family gathered. The half-term holiday began yesterday, so there's no school for several days, no pressure, no other people. There will just be chilling around the house, lots of hugs and family time and answering all their questions.

A box of tissues sits on the table and every single member of the family has taken one. It's been an intense half hour, carefully planned and scripted and discussed by Eve and Nick for weeks.

"You know Mummy had an operation," their little

speech had begun. "And you know she's been ill. Well, her illness is a form of cancer."

And so the speech went on, until Nick's eyes were glistening and Izzy was fully crying and even John was reaching for a tissue.

Five children. Five bundles of love. And five bundles of grief.

Can you call it grief? Nothing's happened yet. She feels fit and strong. She's recovered well from surgery; she can walk again; she's undergoing treatments. But the cancer she's been stricken with is incurable and aggressive, with scary survival statistics.

Maybe "pre-grief" is a better term. Or there again, maybe all of this is overkill. Unnecessary. Her optimism surfaces again. A cure will be found. Her scans will be clear as a bell for years and years. They'll laugh about it one day. *Do you remember when we thought you had incurable cancer?*

But, "You must tell the children," the oncologist had said, and he was God, after all. And the worst thing would be if their children heard a clumsy version from someone else. Some well-meaning friend or neighbor. *I'm sorry your mother is so ill.* Or, even worse, playground gossip: *Is your mummy going to die?*

It's not a secret exactly, this cancer of hers, but it's not something she's spread to the whole world, yet it's amazing how many people have spotted her in the street and texted Nick. *Eve's looking very thin, is she OK?*

And so they've got used to breaking the news to others—and thus being reminded of how shocking it is. The truth is that to some extent they've already normalized it in their own lives. The doctors and the pills and the appointments at the cancer center. They've got used to it. They can even joke about it, when they're not crying.

It's only when they see the reactions of friends to the news that they remember how unusual and shocking this new reality of theirs is.

And so they formulated their little speech for the children carefully—not too scaremongering but not too glib either. Realistic yet optimistic and full of hope, which is basically how Eve feels when she's not racked with guilt.

"They will ask lots of questions," the counselor had told Eve and Nick. "They might ask the same questions again and again. You will have to be patient."

"Don't worry," Eve had replied, raising a half smile.

"Nick's used to that. I ask him the same questions every day."

Now she looks around at her beloved children's faces, wondering if they're OK, hoping that they're resilient, wondering as she does approximately every five minutes how much longer she has on this earth and feeling—yet again—an overpowering guilt.

She has read about the stages of grief and can identify in particular with denial. For great tranches of time, she can be in denial. She goes about her day, she does her exercises, she watches TV. Only her constant fatigue gives away the fact that anything is wrong. That and the memory loss, but she was never good at remembering things anyway.

Then she'll read a headline about cancer, or just see her pills on the bathroom counter top, and her diagnosis will come back to her in a terrible whoosh. It seems surreal. It can't be her.

"If you've got brain cancer, how can you speak?" asks Isobel. "How can your brain still work?"

"Luckily I kept the speaking bit of my brain," answers Eve. "And I kept the silly-jokes bit. But one thing that *does* happen now is, I keep losing my phone."

This raises an almost-laugh. Eve is renowned within her own family for constantly losing her phone.

"You always lost your phone anyway!" says Isobel, her trembling voice on the edge between tears and laughter.

"You think having cancer is an excuse?" says Leo, and Eve looks at him gratefully because he's following her lead, trying to find the funny in a ghastly situation.

"Might they find a cure?" asks Arthur, the fifteen-year-old.

"They might, darling," says Eve. "Everything is possible. They're trying new things all the time. But they don't have one at the moment."

Isobel gives a sudden sob and Eve feels the heat of tears springing to her own eyes. "I know," she soothes Isobel, reaching over to rub her back. "I know, my love. It's hard."

I may never see you grow up, my beautiful girl, and I can't bear it.

"It's unfair," Isobel manages between sobs, scrubbing her face with a tissue. "It isn't fair. Why did you get it?"

"I don't know, my darling, and I know it's unfair."

"But you're healthy," puts in Reggie. "I mean, all you ever eat is bean salad."

This is another family in-joke and there's another ripple of almost-laughter.

"The doctor said this cancer isn't due to that kind of thing," says Eve. "It's just down to good or bad luck and I've had bad luck. I've been lucky in so many ways over my life—and this is where I've had bad luck instead. But at the same time, I *am* lucky. I can walk and talk and, look, even play Scrabble. Lots of people in my situation can't."

"You can't *win* at Scrabble, though, Mum," says John, heroically lightening the mood. "Because I'm going to win."

"*I'm* going to win," Arthur contradicts him.

"*I'm* going to win," says Leo. "I've already got the most epic word."

"*I'm* going to win," chimes in Reggie, not to be outdone. "Because I'm awesome."

The mood has lightened even more, and Eve glances at Nick. He gives her a tiny wink and she can tell he's thinking the same as her—they've got through the worst of it.

"Isobel, did you have another question?" asks Eve, seeing that Isobel wants to talk. "You can ask anything you like."

"Yes, I do have a question," says Isobel. "Only I think I know the answer already."

"Ask anything," says Eve, remembering something the counselor said. "It doesn't matter if anyone knows the answer, it can be good to ask the question anyway. And then we can all think about it and talk about it, maybe."

"OK," says Isobel. "Well, here's my question. Is 'yit' a word?"

Eve feels a jolt of surprise, followed by a flood of immense relief. Isobel is already thinking about Scrabble. She's already bouncing back.

"'Yit'?" echoes Arthur derisively. "What's that supposed to mean?"

"It's a boat," asserts Isobel with a degree of bravado.

"You mean 'yacht.'"

"No, yit! I'm sure a yit is a kind of boat."

"Use it in a sentence," says John, and Isobel takes a deep breath.

"He sailed there in his yit."

The whole family collapses in laughter, and Eve feels almost buoyant. If you glanced in through the window, you'd see a normal, happy family, gathered around a

Scrabble board in the kitchen, all laughing, with not a care in the world.

She knows she'll plummet in spirits again—they'll all plummet in spirits again at some time. But right now she's smiling and her family are laughing and it's all right. Just for now, it's all right.

All the Kind Emails

Dearest Eve and Nick, I am so very sorry . . . we were so very shocked . . . hear the news of Eve . . . must be so frightening . . . always seemed so healthy . . . anything we can do . . . keeping you in our prayers . . . help with the children in any way . . . do anything at all . . . take you out for a drink one evening . . . send you a small gift . . . visit . . . anything we can do . . . thinking of you, thinking of you, thinking of you . . .

Dearest friends, Thank you so much for the wonderful flowers . . . delicious fruit basket . . . interesting article

*you sent . . . inspiring book you sent . . . gorgeous body
lotion you sent . . . Eve sends you so many thanks and
love and is doing very well . . . Thanks for picking up
Isobel . . . thanks for having Reggie to sleep over . . .
thanks for the delicious deli treats . . . visit when Eve's
feeling a bit stronger . . . thanks so much, thanks so
much, thanks so much . . .*

All the Plastic Chairs

"Hi, it's Eve Monroe, here for blood tests."

"Of course, if you could just run your eyes over this form and sign at the bottom? Then please take a seat on one of those plastic chairs."

* * *

"Hello, I'm here to see my consultant, Dr. Cunningham. My name is Eve Monroe."

"Very good, if you could just check the form and sign it and then you and your partner can go and sit on those plastic chairs."

Sophie Kinsella

* * *

"Hello, I'm here for radiation therapy."

"No problem. If I can give you this form to look over
and sign, then just take a seat on those plastic chairs and
we'll be ready for you shortly."

* * *

"Hello, I'm Eve Monroe, I'm here to pick up chemotherapy drugs."

"Absolutely. We will process this as quickly as we can.
Meanwhile, please go and sit on those plastic chairs."

* * *

"Hello, it's Eve Monroe for an MRI scan."

"Of course. Please fill in this safety questionnaire,
then take a seat on the plastic chairs over there."

* * *

"Hello, it's Eve Monroe for the plastic chairs. Sorry, I
mean, for a flat white."

It Could Be Worse

"Are you getting enough sleep?" asks the doctor, and Eve draws breath to answer.

I crawl into bed at eight o'clock, tired out and nauseous and longing for oblivion. I wake up twelve hours later, or thirteen or fourteen. I am greedy for sleep, I want only sleep. I seek unconsciousness like a crack addict seeking a hit.

"Oh yes, I think so," she says. "Plenty, thanks."

"And while you're taking the chemo, do you have any sickness?"

I feel like my insides are pulverizing themselves into smithereens. I feel polluted and poisoned and ready to turn myself inside out. My skin feels sick. My hair feels sick. I have never known a feeling like this.

"I feel a bit sick sometimes," says Eve. "But it could be worse."

"What about fatigue?"

I feel dead like a corpse. I feel like I can't even move my little finger. My body weighs a ton and every thought is exhausting.

"I feel a bit tired sometimes," says Eve. "But it could be worse."

"What about mentally? How's your mood?"

I cycle through denial, despair, shock, grief, and then sometimes ridiculous happiness. I appreciate small pleasures so much more than I did, but then along comes the brutal knowledge again. Sometimes I contemplate dying and leaving my family and I can't bear it. I wait until the house is empty, then cry ugly sobs, inconsolable, loud, keening and wailing, punching the bed with ineffectual, powerless fists. . . .

"Oh, up and down," says Eve after a long pause. "But, you know. It could be worse."

How to Get Through Cancer Treatments

A friendly guide by Eve Monroe

The way to get through radiotherapy: Pretend you are at a fancy spa. So when you are checking in at reception, pretend you are checking in for your spa treatment. And when you are asked to change into a gown, pretend it is a fluffy robe. And when you're asked to lie down on a piece of machinery, pretend it's a high-tech piece of state-of-the-art equipment for facials. (Apparently Gwyneth Paltrow uses it, so it must be good.)

And when they come and pin your head down firmly with the bespoke blue plastic mask so that you can't move a muscle, pretend it is a fancy facial device.

The radiotherapy nurses will talk above your head in a kind of technical jargon. Pretend they are Spanish facialists discussing your skin type in Spanish.

Then, when the radiotherapy actually begins, switch tack, still channeling Gwyneth. All the way through, tell yourself that this treatment will flood your brain with healing and vanish any remaining cancerous debris. Manifest it to be true. Will it to be true. Make it be true.

Don't think about the bald patch that this treatment will undoubtedly give you. Bald patches are not very Gwyneth.

Before you know it, the therapists will be back, unpinning you and asking how you feel.

Sit up, blinking, and think, *I got through that.* And now you just have to get through the next one.

* * *

The way to get through chemotherapy side effects: Do a five-hundred-meter sprint every day, eat only cabbage, meditate, and write a daily gratitude journal to your creator.

I'm joking. The way to get through chemotherapy side effects: Go to bed.

* * *

The way to get through an MRI scan: Don't move. Pretend the noise is some piece of contemporary music or building works next door. Send positive, healing thoughts to your brain with mantras—e.g., *My scan is clean, the disease has not progressed*—in the hope that this will affect the result. (If your mind drifts to the Sweaty Betty sale instead, do not beat yourself up.)

* * *

The way to get through scanxiety: Is there a way? Please let me know what it is.

Early-Morning Conversations 1: Death

"You have to be there when I die." Without warning, a maelstrom of fear and angst has descended upon Eve on waking. Is she ready for death? Should she be? Or is contemplating death the same as giving up hope?

"Be there when?" asks Nick blearily. "What time is it? It's early."

"Sorry," says Eve in rising distress. "I just . . . I just need to know you'll be there when I die. I need to hear your voice. Your voice relaxes me. Plus, you need to tell me what to do and where to go. You know me—I haven't got any sense of direction. I'll end up in the wrong place."

Nick roars with laughter, rubbing his eyes.

"You'll end up in the wrong place because you didn't have your sat nav on you."

"Really, though," she says, her voice tense with nerves. "You can't leave me at the end. I have to hear your voice."

"Of course I'll be there. But you're not going to die for a million years, so we've got time to plan. Anyway, you'll probably outlive me, so it'll be the other way around."

There's a pause, then Eve draws breath.

"Seriously," she says in a different voice. "Nick, have you thought about it? Me going?"

There's another, longer pause.

"Yes, I've thought about it," Nick says at last, also in a different voice. "Of course I have."

"I need to make a will."

"You've got a will. But we do need to talk about a few things, when you're up to it."

"Another will, then. And plans. And arrangements. I need to plan my funeral," says Eve in a fervent rush. "That's a priority."

"Do you, though?"

"Of course! It's not fair to leave it all to you. I'll choose the music and everything. The hymns and the readings. What else do you have at funerals?"

"Eve, it's only five A.M.," observes Nick. "D'you think we've got time for a cup of tea before we finalize your funeral arrangements?"

She knows he is teasing her and she gives a reluctant laugh, but the maelstrom is still there in her head. She's terrified, only she's not quite sure what she's terrified of.

"I have to hear your voice at the end," she says. "Please promise me that."

"I promise," says Nick, and reaches over to hug her. "But it isn't going to happen for a long time. Let's believe that."

"And still make arrangements."

"We can do both. We can both plan a funeral and at the same time believe we won't need the plan for years and years. Win-win. Schrödinger's funeral."

"OK," says Eve. "Let's do that."

"And now I'm going to make a cup of tea," says Nick, getting out of bed. "Why don't you try to go back to sleep? And then we can plan your funeral, your memorial, your will, your life insurance, and all the other sexy stuff."

"I'm serious," says Eve.

"I know," says Nick. "Me too."

"Life used to be more fun," says Eve.

"Yes." He nods soberly. "Agreed."

"Cancer is a buzzkill, what with the pills and the chemo and the dying."

"Yes," says Nick thoughtfully. "It's a fucker. But *luckily . . .*"

Eve laughs, because "luckily" is their family watch word. Tack it on to any gloomy sentence, they have instructed their children, and you can turn things around, viz:

It's raining. But *luckily,* we've all got umbrellas.

I hate hockey. But *luckily,* I also play football.

I have incurable cancer. But *luckily,* my last scan was good.

"*Luckily,*" reiterates Nick, "there's always a cup of tea."

"There's always a cup of tea," agrees Eve. "And sometimes there's toast as well. Life doesn't get much better than that, does it?"

Her maelstrom has ebbed away. She's looking forward to her tea. The day has barely begun but already she feels she's learned a little something. She couldn't exactly articulate it . . . already her thoughts are floating away . . . but she knows she's learned it. And that's what counts. Surely.

Early-Morning Conversations 2: To Bucket List or Not to Bucket List

"The Galápagos Islands," says Nick, reading from his phone. "Machu Picchu. Now your legs are strong again, you could do that. Or the pyramids. Very popular."

"I'm not allowed to fly, remember?" says Eve. "And I'm not sure I could face going all the way to the pyramids by train."

"OK, then," says Nick. "Paris. Rome. Bruges. Take the children. Cultural trip."

"Maybe," says Eve consideringly. "I don't really feel like traveling, though. What else does it say?"

"Meet a celebrity."

"I've met celebrities," says Eve, after a moment's thought. "They're not all that. They're just normal people but with more makeup. What else?"

"Skydive."

"Definitely not. What else?"

"Bungee jump."

"Isn't that pretty much the same as a skydive? What else?"

"Get married."

"Done," says Eve regretfully. "It's a shame, because planning a wedding would be a really good distraction. I could always get remarried, I suppose. Meet someone cute in the cancer center and fall in love. And then I could write the novel *We Met in the Chemo Queue*."

"'Write a novel' is on the list, actually," says Nick, peering at his phone. "But I think you've got that covered. It also says, 'Seek out sensory pleasures, or return to those you have enjoyed in the past.' Shall I book you a massage?"

"I'd like to find a really good marmalade," says Eve thoughtfully. "Like that delicious stuff we ate in Italy."

Nick roars with laughter. "Better marmalade. Is that your bucket list? Are you Paddington Bear?"

Eve laughs in turn. "Maybe I don't want a bucket list at all. I think what I want is just to live like we do anyway—you know, do our work and go for walks and watch *Come Dine with Me*—but have a slightly nicer version of it. Normal but better. Call it 'Normal plus.'"

"'Normal plus,'" says Nick. "I like that. Let's aim for normal plus in everything we do. So when we go out to see a film, we upgrade to slightly nicer cinema tickets."

"Exactly. And we eat nicer food than we would have done normally."

"When we watch *Come Dine with Me*, we have exotic snacks," suggests Nick, "and therefore elevate the experience."

"Exactly." Eve laughs. "We eat kiwi fruit and mango slices. Get us!"

"So your bucket list is basically marmalade, kiwi fruit, mango, and *Come Dine with Me*," comments Nick. "You're not very demanding, are you? I was waiting to plan the whole skydiving Machu Picchu holiday."

"Seriously?" Eve laughs.

"Seriously," says Nick, his face suddenly grave. "Anything you want to do, Eve. Anything. I will make it happen. From mango to Machu Picchu to . . . I don't know. Fly to the Space Station."

"OK, here's the thing," says Eve honestly. "I've done a lot of exciting, bucket-listy stuff in my life. I've done glamorous travel and I've walked the red carpet and I've swum with dolphins. I don't need to do any more of that stuff. I just need to be around. Have fun with the children. Have fun with you. See friends. Small pleasures."

"Are you calling *Come Dine with Me* a small pleasure?" says Nick in mock outrage.

"Well, obviously not. It's the hugest pleasure of my life." Eve laughs again. "But you know what I mean."

"I know what you mean." He nods. "Normal plus."

"Normal plus." She picks up the iPad and starts typing briskly while Nick watches her with curiosity.

"What are you doing?" he asks.

"I'm starting on my bucket list, of course," she says, and smiles at him. "I'm browsing posh marmalade."

Early-Morning Conversations 3: The Early Signs

"Everyone who has cancer writes an article," observes Eve one day, flicking through the *Daily Mail*. "They get cancer and then they write an article saying, 'These were the early signs of my cancer' and they warn people. Look, here's one called 'The Five Deadly Signs of a Brain Tumor.' Should I write a piece like that?"

"Maybe," says Nick. "You could do."

"Except I don't know what they are," says Eve, scanning the article. "Apart from headaches. What were my early signs anyway? How did you guess I had something really wrong with me?"

For Eve, the story begins when she was already in hospital. That's her first memory of this whole roller coaster: waking up in a hospital bed and not knowing what was going on and being told she was going to have a scan of her brain.

"You started lurching around," says Nick. "You couldn't walk. You were staggering everywhere, and leaning to one side, even when you were sitting in a chair."

"Did I change personality?" queries Eve. "It says here, 'Sign Four: changes in personality, e.g., becoming moody and bitter.' Am I moody and bitter?"

Nick laughs. "Not moody or bitter. Yet."

"But this means that if I act moody or bitter, it's not my fault," says Eve, in sudden realization. "I have a free pass to change personality however I like. Excellent. I think I'll be obnoxious and demanding."

"You did go a bit haywire," volunteers Nick. "Before you had the scan. You wanted to cut all your hair off."

"Cut my *hair* off?" says Eve in disbelief.

"You got the scissors and told me to do it in the kitchen. You kept saying, 'Chop it all off.' I didn't know what to do."

"Oh my God," breathes Eve. "That's unreal." Then she

gives a sudden giggle. "Wait, Nick. You do realize you're basically describing me after a girls' night out? Staggering around, falling off my chair, and saying I need to change my haircut."

"Fair enough!" Nick starts laughing too. "Now you mention it . . ."

"In fact, are we sure this whole thing was a brain tumor?" Eve gives another giggle. "Maybe it was just a really bad hangover. In fact, that could be the article I write for the *Mail*. I could call it 'Brain Tumor or Hangover? Your Handy Checklist.'"

"'Tumor or Tequila?'" Nick joins in, and Eve laughs again, almost hysterically. She hasn't laughed properly for ages; she almost thought she'd forgotten how to.

"No wonder they won't let me drive anymore," she says, between giggles. "But anyway, tell me more, because I don't remember what happened. I staggered around and fell off my chair, so they gave me an MRI scan."

"Exactly."

"And then you knew I had a growth, but you didn't know it was cancerous."

"I didn't officially know it was cancerous, but . . ." He hesitates. "I knew. When they asked me into a little side room, I guessed something was up. Then, when the doctor told me they'd found something, I knew it was bad news."

"How?" she asks, intrigued.

"Because . . ." Nick pauses as though wondering whether to continue, then draws breath. "Because he was in tears."

"In *tears*?" Something heavy seems to thud inside Eve and her giggles melt away.

"He was in tears." Nick nods, and a blanket of silence seems to descend upon them.

"What happened next?" whispers Eve.

"Then they had to decide whether to operate or not. Which they did. And then we just needed to get you fit for surgery."

"'Strong for surgery,'" quotes Eve, having a sudden vague memory. "What do they call it? Prehab."

"That's right. You did sessions with the physio and you did get strong. You *are* strong. So that's good."

Nick sounds positive, because he always does, but his face is taut, as though he's remembering difficult things, and Eve's whole heart wrenches with grief.

"This is harder for you than it is for me," she says suddenly, her eyes spilling over with tears again. "It's harder for you."

"Don't be silly," says Nick at once. "It's harder for you. You're the one with the illness."

"But you're the one who . . . if I die . . . looking after the children . . ." She wipes her eyes. "I mean, it'll be easy for me, won't it? I'll be dead. You have the hardest side of this."

"OK," says Nick after a long pause. "Well, let's say it's hard for both of us."

Fresh tears run down Eve's face as she imagines Nick, all alone, sitting in a little hospital side room, having to deal with the news that his wife had a deadly brain tumor, and she feels sudden rage. Rage at her own stupid brain; rage at the doctor for upsetting Nick; rage at the whole thing. She wants to rail and shout and hit things. And she feels—yet again—consumed by guilt that she has been the cause of so much distress. She knows this cancer is not her fault—it's just bad luck. But what she has learned is that you can feel guilty for having had bad luck.

And so the guilt and rage storm around her brain. But at the same time, she feels quite calm, because what's she going to do? It is what it is. And it could be worse. She could be dead already.

"Maybe I'll call my piece, 'Want a New Haircut? You Might Have Cancer,'" she says, trying to sound normal. "I'm sure some newspaper will buy that."

"Definitely." He smiles and she gives a watery smile back, and they squeeze hands, tight. And they manage not to talk about it again for almost another hour.

Early-Morning Conversations
4: All the Ironies

"You realize how ironic it is?" says Eve early another morning, shifting her head on her pillow.

"What's ironic?" inquires Nick sleepily.

"Well, first of all, let's agree that I am Eve Monroe, queen of happy endings."

"Agreed," says Nick. "You are queen of happy endings. Happy endings bought this house." He gestures around. "We're very grateful to happy endings."

"I was once doing a bookshop event," Eve says reminiscently, "and the interviewer asked, 'Would you ever try writing something different?' I answered, 'Maybe I'll write a book with a sad ending'—just as a joke, really—and a woman in the front row shrieked 'No!' in total panic. It was very funny."

Nick laughs. "Your readers love happy endings."

"Of course they do. I love happy endings myself. So I've invented lots of them. But now here's the irony: I can't invent a real-life happy ending for myself."

"That's very ironic," agrees Nick. "What would your real-life happy ending look like?"

"Let me think a moment," says Eve, then draws breath. "OK, I'll pitch it to you. A clinical trial in Ottawa suddenly produces a miracle cure involving cannabis oil, just in time for the heroine to use it and become fully cured, surrounded by her joyful family. I'd cast George Clooney as the brilliant but misunderstood oncologist, and I'd be played by Emily Blunt. The children could play themselves."

"Why cannabis oil?"

Eve shrugs. "Dunno. It just seems quite 'now.'"

"Why Ottawa?"

"So that there's a dash through an airport. Everyone loves a dash through the airport."

"OK. Well, that's a good ending," says Nick. "I like it."

"I like it too." Eve nods. "It would be a nice positive

twist, just at the end of the story when everyone's given up hope."

"I haven't given up hope," says Nick. "Just so you know."

"No, I haven't either," says Eve. "But people do give up hope. Gloomy people."

For a while they're both quiet and there's silence in the room except for some thumping from Arthur's room, which is right above theirs. He has taken to lifting weights, and the thumps are a regular occurrence.

"Here's another irony for you," she says. "My brain was the secret of my success when I was writing books. But now my brain's the very thing causing all the problems."

"Your brain has no sense of moderation," agrees Nick. "It's either doing brilliant things or bloody stupid things."

"Yes." Eve nods. "It's a ridiculous brain. I just wish I had more control over it. Then I could write my own happy ending and make it happen for real."

There's quiet again, broken by the sound of music from Arthur's room, accompanied by still more thumps.

"You know what else is ironic?" says Nick.

"What?"

"You hate spoilers in books and films. We both do. But when it comes to this, all we want, above anything else, is a spoiler. We desperately want the doctors to give us the spoiler, but they can't, because they don't know either."

"Yes!" exclaims Eve. "Exactly. I want to *know*. I'm a novelist. I'm used to being God. I decide on the ending before I begin."

"Sometimes you change your mind," points out Nick.

"Yes, but the point is, I'm the boss. I'm in charge of my whole universe. Whereas in real life . . ."

"You're not the boss anymore."

"Apparently not. Fate's the boss. And there are no teasers. All we can do is wait and see what happens."

"Every scan is a plot twist."

"Exactly!" exclaims Eve. "Every scan is a plot twist. When's my next scan again?" she adds, feeling a sudden twinge of nerves.

"Three weeks to go."

"Three weeks to wait until the plot unfolds again . . . And no spoilers."

"No," says Nick, kissing her. "No spoilers. More's the pity."

WhatsApp

Eve's Family Support Group

Dearest Eve, Congratulations on
one year on from surgery, you made
it, well done!!!
Mum xxx

Dear Eve
Happy Craniversary!!! See you soon
to celebrate properly . . .
Ginnie xxx

Darling Eve
You made a year! You're nailing
this!!! Heaps of love
Imogen xxx

Happy Ending

It's fourteen months since diagnosis—and the main point is, she's still here. She's had another "stable" scan: her fourth now. Four stable scans is good. Four feels substantial.

She's finished chemo, she feels well, she has a lot more energy, she's even started writing again. Is anything actually still wrong? It all seems unbelievable.

So energetic is she these days that Nick has booked the whole family on a charity walk. The T-shirts arrive through the post, each one bright red with THE BRAIN TUMOUR CHARITY printed in white, and on the appointed day they all dress up in T-shirts, trainers, and joggers.

The sun is shining as they reach the London church where the walk will begin. There are crowds of people in red T-shirts, red balloons everywhere, and on a stage with a PA system, a man in a red T-shirt is mid-speech.

"I would like to thank each and every one of you for being here today," he is saying. "You are supporting research and helping improve essential care and support for those with brain tumors. Together, we can make sure no one faces this diagnosis alone."

As Eve looks around, she is bowled over by how many people are there—some in family groups, some alone, some holding up cards with names. *Joanna. Simon. Mum.* All these other families affected by the same piece of wretched bad luck.

It warms her, to think of herself as part of a community, even if it's not a community she would have chosen to join. She takes a family selfie and hopes that this day will be a precious memory for her children. The day they put something back; the day they all came together for a good cause.

"So finally, thank you again for turning out," says the

man on the stage. "Enjoy the walk and see you at the finish line! Three, two, one—GO!"

The crowd surges off down the London streets to the sound of klaxons and cheering, and soon makes a stream of red T-shirts moving through Hyde Park. The pace is brisk and Eve feels exhilarated at being part of it.

"I'm walking the red carpet again," she says to Nick with a laugh, gesturing around at the sea of red T-shirts. "Do you remember when I was on a Zimmer frame? It seems ages ago now."

"You've done amazingly."

"I feel normal. I feel like there's nothing wrong with me at all. Maybe it's all been a big mistake."

She's taking cannabis oil now, as recommended by her oncologist, and that makes her feel uplifted too. Maybe her fictitious happy ending will come true, although probably without George Clooney.

As she strides along, faster and faster, she feels a sudden wave of optimism. Everything seems possible. Of *course* she'll see the children grow up. Of *course* she'll meet her grandchildren. Of *course* she'll write more books. Of *course* she'll get back on the tennis court.

If she can walk 10K, then why shouldn't she beat the

odds? She's been super-lucky in life...then super-unlucky...so maybe the next swing will be toward luck.

"Keep going!" shouts a nearby walk marshal in a red T-shirt. "You're doing really well! Keep going!"

"OK!" Eve shouts back happily. "I'll keep going!"

And right at that moment, this is her only aim in life, the only happy ending she wants. Just to keep going.

Author's Note

What Does It Feel Like? is fiction, but it is my most auto-biographical work to date. Eve's story is my story.

In the autumn of 2022, I began to feel ill—and my early signs of cancer were the same as Eve's. From the staggering through the wheelchair, the Zimmer frame, surgery, diagnosis, and beyond, it all happened pretty much as is set down in these pages. I even asked my husband, Henry, to cut all my hair off. (I don't remember this, but he says I was pretty insistent!)

I underwent an eight-hour operation to remove my glioblastoma tumor, and went through subsequent chemotherapy and radiotherapy. I learned to walk again, to balance again, to move my head again and function again. Like Eve, I was very distressed that I couldn't remember any Christmas carols, and I furiously memorized them again in time for Christmas.

Why did I fictionalize my story? In a strange way, it liberated me to be honest and raw. I have five children: Freddy, Hugo, Oscar, Rex, and Sybella. Somehow it was easier to write about them honestly using fictional names. I felt free to change details and make the story work as best I could.

Because, although it is autobiographical, not every detail in this book is true. Some events happened in a different order or I have altered them slightly. But all inventions are minor and don't change the essential truth of the story.

I will give you one example. I did indeed once buy a Jenny Packham sequined dress in a Wimbledon Village boutique when I was supposed to be writing, and I did indeed get caught out when Henry phoned to see how the writing was going and I was halfway into the dress. I did indeed say, "If you buy the dress, the occasion will come," which I firmly believe to this day. I eventually wore the dress to a party at the Ivy given for me by my agent, and I felt like a princess. However, to the *Shopaholic* premiere I wore a pink Alexander McQueen dress. But for this book, the sequined dress seemed "meant to be" as Eve's premiere outfit, so that's how I wrote it. This is the luxury of fiction—you are in complete control. You can tweak and alter and no one will point out the inaccuracies. This was also useful because my memory is still very patchy and I sometimes had to invent where I had no recollection.

Attentive readers will notice that the style of this book is different from my normal novels, and again, this just was the most natural way for me to tell the story. It poured out of me in the form of vignettes and snippets and slices of life; somehow I couldn't tell it in any other way.

Why did I write such a personal book?

I am a very private person, so it may seem strange that I have revealed so many raw details of my life to the world. However, I have always processed my life using writing. Hiding behind my fictional characters, I have always turned my own life into a narrative. It is my version of therapy, maybe. Writing is my happy place, and writing this book, although tough going at times, was immensely satisfying and therapeutic for me.

From my engagement on social media, I have come across many readers who are going through similar struggles or challenges to mine and Eve's. I really hope that Eve's optimism might be helpful or inspiring to anyone suffering cancer or another illness or supporting a sufferer.

And finally, I wish everyone reading this a very happy ending.

Sophie Kinsella
April 2024

Acknowledgments

The acknowledgments page is customarily the place where a grateful author acknowledges the help she has had in publishing a novel. However, in this case, I want to start with my gratitude for being alive today—and for that, I need to thank some medical professionals. Professor Andrew McEvoy operated on me when my glioblastoma was first diagnosed. Since then I have been under the care of Dr. Michael Kosmin and Dr. Paul Mulholland. I am grateful to all three professionals for being so kind and for supporting both me and Henry through this difficult time. I would also like to thank the many nurses and other medical staff who have been a great support and help, as well as Dr. Prashanth Reddy and Dr. Charles Middle at the time of my diagnosis.

And now onto my beloved publishing family, who helped this book into the world with such love and care.

Araminta Whitley, Marina de Pass, Nicki Kennedy, and Kim Witherspoon, thank you for representing me; I love you all. Enormous thanks to my publishers, in particular Bill Scott-Kerr, Sarah Adams, Becky Short, Julia Teece, Kim Young, Kate Samano, Whitney Frick, Karen Fink, Debbie Aroff, Avideh Bashirrad, Joy Terekiev, Maria Runge, Andrea Best, and Caroline Ast, for championing this book with such enthusiasm, love, and sensitivity.

The kindness of friends to both me and Henry has blown me away and I would like to thank in particular Stephen and Catherine Nelson, Roger and Clare Barron, Ana-Maria Rincon, Tom and Clare Downes, Jenny Colgan, Jojo Moyes, Lisa Jewell, Jenny Bond, Linda Evans, Hermione Norris, Kirsty Crawford, Nick and Naomi Hewitt, Clare Hedley, Emily Stokely, and Theresa Ward, and everyone else who dropped me a kind message or gift or looked after the children or gave me moral support.

When I was first diagnosed, my family swung into immediate helpful action, much like Eve's family, and I must thank my sisters, Gemma Malley and Abigail Parkhurst, and my mother, Patricia Townley. My children, Freddy, Hugo, Oscar, Rex, and Sybella, have been a continual comfort, and we have all been helped throughout by Carol Vargas. A special mention also to my lovely daughter-in-law, Lizzie.

Several friends have been particularly kind to Henry and we would like to thank Liam Maxwell, Mark Birch, Chris Hancock, Mason Bain, Emma, and Mike.

Some of my readers may be fundraisers through school charities, corporate charities, or private donations. The Brain Tumour Charity is a real organization that does much good, and I encourage you to consider it in your fundraising.

And lastly, to my wonderful readers. Your loyal support has buoyed me up more than I can say and I am incredibly grateful for all the messages of encouragement and support that I have received. Thank you so much and lots of love.

Sophie Kinsella x

About the Author

SOPHIE KINSELLA is a writer and former financial journalist. She is the #1 bestselling author of *Can You Keep a Secret?*, *The Undomestic Goddess*, *Remember Me?*, *Twenties Girl*, *I've Got Your Number*, *Wedding Night*, *My Not So Perfect Life*, *Surprise Me*, *I Owe You One*, *Love Your Life*, *The Party Crasher*, *The Burnout*, the hugely popular Shopaholic novels, and the young adult novel *Finding Audrey*. She lives in the UK with her husband and family.

sophiekinsella.com
X: @KinsellaSophie
Instagram: @sophiekinsellawriter

About the Type

This book was set in Albertina, a typeface created by Dutch calligrapher and designer Chris Brand (1921–98). Brand's original drawings, based on calligraphic principles, were modified considerably to conform to the technological limitations of typesetting in the early 1960s. The development of digital technology later allowed Frank E. Blokland (b. 1959) of the Dutch Type Library to restore the typeface to its creator's original intentions.

Catch up with
SOPHIE KINSELLA

Sign up for Sophie's e-newsletter at
SophieKinsella.com

And don't miss Sophie Kinsella's bestselling Shopaholic series.